SWEETIE

**Don't miss any of these
other stories by Ellen Miles!**

THE PUPPY PLACE

SWEETIE

ELLEN MILES

LITTLE · APPLE

SCHOLASTIC INC.

New York   Toronto   London   Auckland
Sydney   Mexico City   New Delhi   Hong Kong

For Dalton, Maura, Claire, Andrew, Emily, Ula,

Sarah, Ronnie, Karlee, Kristin, Collin,

and all my other #1 readers and incredible fans!

ISBN: 978-0-545-16811-3

Cover art by Tim O'Brien
Original cover design by Steve Scott

12 11 10 9 8 7 6 5 4 3   10 11 12 13 14 15/0

Printed in the U.S.A.

First printing, January 2010

CHAPTER ONE

"Brike five! You're bonked," Charles Peterson shouted at his best friend, Sammy.

"That was no brike. That was a stall!" Sammy yelled back. "Come on." He waved the Wiffle blat over his head and swung at an imaginary boodja. "One more. I'm gonna hit a bipple!"

"Just try!" David was way back in the boutfield, by the rowing machine. He crouched down and jiggled from foot to foot on his tiptoes. He looked ready for anything.

Charles shrugged happily and leaned back to throw. Base-boodja. Did it get any better than this? So what if it was a gloomy Monday in February? Sure, it was cold and gray outside. It wasn't baseball season yet, but it was definitely

1

time for some indoor base-boodja, which was a brand-new game never before played in the history of the world.

Charles was glad that he and Sammy had gotten to know David. When David had first moved to Littleton, not that long ago, he'd seemed really shy. He was still pretty quiet at school, where all three boys were in the same class: Mr. Mason's, Room 2B. David didn't like big groups. But after he and Charles had found a stray dog — and helped it find its way home — David had gotten used to being around Charles. It took a little longer for David to get used to Sammy, because Sammy was, as Charles's dad sometimes said, "a real character" who loved to tell jokes and come up with crazy ideas.

Anyway, now David wasn't shy at all with Charles and Sammy. In fact, sometimes you couldn't get him to *stop* talking. He liked to tell long, detailed stories about things he and his parents had done, like camping out in Yellowstone

National Park and seeing a grizzly bear there. Charles loved David's stories, even though Sammy didn't always believe them.

Base-boodja was invented one day when the boys were all over at David's house. David dug out a yellow Wiffle bat and a big purple Nerf ball. "Mom says we can play in the basement," he reported. "We can make all the noise we want down there."

Charles and Sammy looked at each other. Charles wasn't so sure he liked that idea, and he could tell that Sammy felt the same way. The basement at Charles's house was cold and clammy, with a scary toilet (it made weird gurgling noises) in one corner and the washer and dryer in another. A big clanking furnace was always roaring to life when you least expected it, and there was a permanently moist area on the floor by the outside door.

But David's basement turned out to be different. It was brightly lit and warm and dry, with a

3

giant mirror that took up one whole wall. The best part was that just about the entire floor was covered in thick, spongy blue mats like the ones in the gym at school, so you could jump around, fall down, do somersaults — anything! — without getting hurt. David's mom and dad used the basement as a workout room. The people who had lived in the house before had left behind all sorts of gym equipment. Besides the rowing machine, there was also a treadmill, and some kind of bench with weights you could pull down, and an exercise bike that looked like fun but turned out to be really boring to ride.

Soon the boys took the place over. They played down there on weekends and almost every day after school. David's mom was always popping down the stairs to make sure the boys weren't getting themselves in trouble, and they weren't allowed to play on any of the equipment unless an adult was in the basement with them. But besides that they were pretty much free to do whatever they wanted in that big, safe, padded room.

They were never sure who had actually invented base-boodja. Sammy said he had come up with the name, and David said he was the one who'd thought of the basic rules. It was all so new that the boys were still figuring the game out.

"Okay, instead of three strikes, you get five brikes when you're up at blat," Charles said one day, after his third brike.

"Fine, but if you get five, you're broke," David agreed. "Like, instead of striking out."

Sammy was the one who had come up with the names for all the hits. "A hit to the weight machine is a bingle," he said. "If you slam it to the rowing machine, it's a bubble." He pointed the blat at the bottom of the stairs. "And over there, that's a bipple."

"But if somebody catches a flying boodja —" Charles began.

"Or throws it at you and hits you with it," added David, "then you're bonked — and the next person is up."

Another day, Sammy blasted it all the way past the treadmill. "That's a Grand Boodjerino!" he yelled. "I win the game!" From then on, they all tried their hardest to hit Grand Boodjerinos.

Each boy was like a team of his own, and they kept track of their all-time best scores on the white wipe-off board by the light switches, tallying up every hit they ever made.

Charles was the Jackal. His lifetime score was twenty-six, including three Grand Boodjerinos. David was the Hurricane. He had four Grand Boodjerinos (although Sammy always said one of them didn't count because it had bounced off the back of the treadmill and he had caught it) and a score of twenty-three. And Sammy was the Green-Eyed Alien. He led the league with five Grand Boodjerinos and a high score of twenty-nine.

Charles loved base-boodja. In fact, he thought now, as he wound up to pitch the boodja to Sammy on that gloomy Monday in February, it was almost as much fun as playing with a puppy, Charles's favorite thing in the whole world.

Charles was crazy about puppies. He had one of his own (well, he shared him with his older sister, Lizzie, and his little brother, Adam, who was known as the Bean), an adorable mutt named Buddy. Buddy was brown, with the softest fur ever. He had a white patch in the shape of a heart on his chest, and ears that flopped over in the cutest way, and shiny brown eyes. Buddy was the best thing that had ever happened to Charles. He was huggable and so much fun to play with, and he never, ever told anybody a single one of the secrets that Charles whispered into his ears.

Charles was lucky to have Buddy. But his luck didn't stop there. Charles also got to meet lots of other puppies and take care of them and play with them and teach them manners and tricks.

That was because the Petersons were a foster family for puppies who needed homes. They kept each puppy just long enough to find it the perfect forever family. Taking care of foster puppies could be a lot of work sometimes, but Charles loved it. As soon as one puppy was gone, he began to wonder and dream about the next puppy. Where would it come from? What kind would it be? Charles loved all sorts of puppies: big puppies, little puppies, furry puppies, silly puppies. Lately he had been wishing that his family would get to foster a really big puppy, like a Great Dane. A Great Dane puppy could be bigger than Maggie, a Saint Bernard the Petersons had once fostered — maybe even bigger than the Bean. That would be so cool.

"Yo, Cheese." Sammy swung the blat. "Pitch it, pal!"

Oops. Sometimes Charles got a little carried away when he thought about puppies. He blinked

8

at his friend. *Cheese?* Then he remembered. "Okay, Salami, here it comes."

Cheese and Salami were nicknames Charles and Sammy had made up years ago, long before they met David. Charles had almost forgotten all about them. He wondered why Sammy was calling him that now. Maybe to let David know that Sammy was Charles's first best friend, before David came along?

Charles wound up again and threw. *Bam!* Sammy swung and connected. The boodja blooped toward David, who dove for it, sliding along the blue mat. He caught it on the second bounce and whirled to throw it at Sammy. Sammy did a quick little dance step to avoid the flying boodja and reached out to touch the weight machine. "Bingle!" He threw his arms in the air.

David shook his head disgustedly as he took over the pitcher's mound. Charles ran for the blat and picked it up. He swung a few times to get the feel of it. The blat felt good in his hands. He had a hunch he was about to hit a Grand Boodjerino.

The door to the upstairs opened. "Charles," called David's mother. "Your dad's on the phone. He says he's on his way to pick you up."

"Now?" Charles asked. "But —"

David's mother was on her way down the stairs. She handed the phone to Charles.

"Dad?" Charles asked. "Do I have to come home *now*? We're in the middle of —" He stopped and listened to his dad. "Really? Cool, I'll be ready when you get here." Charles handed the phone back to David's mom. Suddenly, he didn't mind quitting the base-boodja game. He didn't mind at all. "We're getting a new foster puppy!" he announced.

CHAPTER TWO

"Is it a Great Dane?" Charles started in on the questions before he even buckled his seat belt. "Where did the puppy come from? Is it already at our house?"

"Slow down there, pardner." His dad smiled at him. "How about 'Hi, Dad, good to see you'?"

"Hi-Dad-good-to-see-you. So, what about the puppy?"

Dad sighed. "It's kind of a long story. Let's wait till we get home. Rick should be there by then, with the puppy, and he'll explain everything."

"Rick the rookie?" Charles asked.

His dad nodded. "That's right."

Charles's dad was a firefighter. Charles knew everybody on the squad down at the station. He could picture Rick, the newest guy. Rick was tall and strong, with a big loud laugh and a huge bristly mustache. He loved to play practical jokes, and according to Dad, he was the best cook at the station.

"So Rick found a puppy and it needs a home?" Charles asked as Dad pulled into the Petersons' driveway. A black sports car — Rick's car — was already parked there.

"Not exactly." Dad opened his door. "Come on. Let's go in and you can hear the whole story."

When they walked into the kitchen, Charles saw Rick sitting at the table with Mom, Lizzie, and the Bean. The Bean sat next to Rick and stared openmouthed at his mustache. But Rick was not smiling or laughing, and even his mustache looked droopy. The big man sat slumped over, his hands wrapped around a mug of coffee. On Rick's lap was a tiny curly-haired puppy. She sat up with her little paws on the edge of the table. Her fur was a beautiful coppery gold color, like leaves in the fall. She looked back at Charles with the brightest black eyes he had ever seen.

Hello there!

"Is that the puppy?" Charles ran over to see.

"Hey there, Charles. This is Sweetie," said Rick in a flat voice. "She's a poodle."

"A miniature poodle," Lizzie added. "Her color is called apricot. She'll never grow very big at all." Charles knew that Lizzie, who knew everything about dogs, was not exactly a fan of little ones. But how could she resist this cutie?

Charles stood next to Rick and reached out to pat the puppy's little head and stroke her fluffy ears. Her coat was springy and soft. She felt delicate, like a fancy piece of china that might break if you even *looked* at it the wrong way.

"Want to hold her?"

Charles nodded. He sat down and Rick handed the puppy over. "Oh!" said Charles. Sweetie had to weigh even less than David's purple Nerf ball. She wasn't much bigger than the Nerf ball, either! Charles held her up to his face to get a closer look, and Sweetie stuck out her tiny pink tongue and licked his cheek, putting one soft little paw on his chin.

Charles smiled. It had taken only one second for him to fall in love with Sweetie. She wasn't a Great Dane puppy, but she was definitely a very special girl. "Why does she need a home?" he asked. He could not imagine why anybody would give this adorable puppy away.

Rick heaved a long, loud sigh. "Sweetie was supposed to be a Valentine's present for my girlfriend, Karen." He stopped and sighed again.

Charles knew that Valentine's Day was only a week or so away. He had already picked out the cards he was going to give to his friends. They were good ones, the funny kind, with cartoon dogs and cats. Charles waited for Rick to go on, but the big man just sat there with his face in his hands.

"So, what? Your girlfriend doesn't like poodles?"

Rick shook his head sadly. "No. She doesn't like *me* anymore, that's what. Karen broke up with me last week. And now I'm stuck with this puppy that I'm not allowed to keep in my apartment."

Lizzie gasped. "This is exactly why it's never a good idea to give a pet for a present," she said. "Ms. Dobbins says that the shelter is packed every year after Christmas with pets that people didn't really want. She says —"

"Lizzie." Mom reached out and grabbed Lizzie's hand. "That's enough."

Charles knew that Lizzie was probably right. Ms. Dobbins was the director of Caring Paws, the shelter where Lizzie volunteered every week. She knew all about unwanted dogs and cats. But it wouldn't do Rick any good to hear Lizzie lecture about it.

"We can help." Charles looked from his dad to his mom. "Right? We can take Sweetie and find her a home, can't we?"

"Help!" echoed the Bean. "We can help."

"Well," said Mom, "what if she turns into a spoiled little dog, like Princess?"

"Not all little dogs are spoiled," said Charles. Anyway, so what if Princess was spoiled? Charles had loved the little Yorkshire terrier his family had fostered. And he'd even found her a wonderful forever family. He sent his dad a pleading look.

Rick sighed again. "Well, if you can't take her, I'm sure I can figure something else out," he began. He reached over to take Sweetie from Charles.

Charles snuggled Sweetie in his arms. "Please, please, please can we keep her?" He did not want to give Sweetie up. She was unlike any other puppy he'd known, with her curly reddish-gold hair and bright eyes. He wanted to foster this tiny puppy. "I promise to take good care of her!"

CHAPTER THREE

Finally, Mom smiled. "Okay, Charles. You and Lizzie have been so responsible with our foster puppies." She turned to Rick. "We'll be happy to take care of Sweetie. She's such a little thing. How much trouble could she be?"

"Yay!" yelled Charles and Lizzie and the Bean. Sweetie's head popped up and she looked all around.

What's all the noise about? Is it a party? I love parties!

The pup scrambled out of Charles's arms and jumped up onto the table.

"Oh, dear," said Mom. "I don't think —" But then she burst out laughing as Sweetie danced toward her.

Dad laughed, too. "The little cutie." He wiped his eyes.

Even Rick cracked a smile. "She's real smart, this one. Only six months old, and she already knows some tricks. The lady I bought her from taught her."

"Tricks? Like what?" Lizzie asked.

"Let's see," said Rick. "She knows how to sit —"

No sooner was the word out of his mouth than Sweetie sat, perching on the table like a tiny statue of a poodle. She cocked her head at Rick.

That was easy. What's next?

Everybody laughed and clapped.

"More," yelled the Bean. "More tricks!"

Rick lifted Sweetie off the table and set her down on the floor. "Roll over, Sweetie," he said.

Sweetie dropped onto her tummy and — quick as a flash — rolled over and bounced back onto her feet.

"Wow!" Even Lizzie, who had taught lots of puppies lots of tricks, was impressed.

"The lady was starting to teach her how to do a backflip, but I think she's still a little young for that." Rick squatted down next to the tiny puppy, looking proud. "She'll jump up onto anything, though." He patted his knee. "Sweetie, up!"

Sweetie sprang up onto Rick's knee. Then he patted the seat of a nearby chair. "Sweetie, up." Sweetie sailed right up onto the chair. Rick was about to pat the table when Mom cleared her throat and shook her head.

"No more dogs on the kitchen table," she said. But she smiled. "Sweetie is a very talented puppy."

"I know," said Rick. "Karen would have loved her." Suddenly, his mustache went all droopy again, and the spark left his eyes. "I love dogs. I wish I could keep Sweetie, but even if she were allowed in my apartment, I think having her around would just be a reminder of how much I miss Karen."

Dad put his hand on Rick's shoulder. "We'll take good care of her. And we'll find her a good home, too. You can count on that."

Rick sniffed and nodded. "Thanks. You don't know how much I appreciate it. One thing: When you're looking for a new owner, make sure that person understands that poodles have to be groomed. The lady I got her from was very clear about that. It's a real commitment to have a poo-dle and pay for a shampoo and some clipping every six to ten weeks."

"I know about that," said Lizzie. "They have to be groomed because poodles have hair, not fur like other dogs. That's why some people who are allergic to dogs can be around poodles without sneezing. Instead of shedding, poodle hair just grows and grows and grows."

Rick nodded. "That's right." He gave Lizzie a weak smile. "I promise I'll never try to give a puppy as a present again. I've learned my lesson."

The big man scooped up the tiny puppy and nuzzled her ears. "Good-bye, Sweetie. You be a good girl." Sweetie looked tinier than ever nestled in his big hands. She licked his cheek, and Rick kissed her on the nose. Then he handed Sweetie over to Charles and walked quickly out of the room, without looking back.

Charles kissed Sweetie between the ears. "We'll take care of you," he said. He turned to Lizzie. "Where's Buddy? Let's see if they get along."

"I put him in my bedroom until Sweetie got comfortable with all of us," said Lizzie. She went to get Buddy while Charles and the Bean took Sweetie into the living room to play. Charles put the puppy down on the rug and watched as she ran around sniffing everything. She tried to pick up one of Buddy's stuffed toys, but it was almost bigger than she was. She tugged and growled, trying to pull Mr. Duck out of the toy basket.

Just then Lizzie came back downstairs, with Buddy trotting after her.

"Uh-oh," said Charles. Mr. Duck was one of Buddy's favorite toys. Maybe he wouldn't be happy to find another puppy playing with it.

But Buddy ran right over to Sweetie, wagging his tail. He pulled Mr. Duck out of the basket and laid him down in front of Sweetie.

Here you go.

Buddy bowed down, his front paws stretched way out.

Want to play?

Sweetie bowed back — and they were off, racing around the room. After a few laps, Buddy rolled over and let Sweetie climb on him. He must have looked like a mountain to the tiny golden brown pup.

"Wow," said Charles. "Everybody loves Sweetie."

"Evvybody love Sweetie," echoed the Bean. He laughed his googly laugh. "The Bean love Sweetie, Charles love Sweetie, Lizzie love Sweetie, Buddy love Sweetie! Dada and Mama love Sweetie!"

Sweetie looked up, one minuscule foot planted on Buddy's chest, and cocked her head.

Of course! And I love you all, too.

Charles laughed. Sweetie was so cute. "Up, Sweetie!" He patted his knee. Sweetie scampered over and jumped, sailing through the air like a little ball of fluff. She landed perfectly on Charles's lap. "Good girl." He gave her a big kiss on the top of her head.

That was when Buddy started to bark.

CHAPTER FOUR

"What's the matter, Buddy?" Charles asked.

Buddy planted both front feet on the carpet and faced Charles, barking like a maniac.

Why does she get to be on your lap? What about me? What about me? What about me?

"I think somebody's jealous." Lizzie raised her eyebrows and pointed at Buddy. "That's never happened before." She went over to pat Buddy. "It's okay, honey. We love you just as much as always."

But Buddy barked until Charles put Sweetie back down on the floor. After that, he played nicely with Sweetie — as long as she stayed away from his people. Every time Sweetie trotted over to Lizzie or tried to kiss the Bean or even *looked* at Charles, Buddy started to bark.

"What's going on in here?" Mom stood in the doorway, her arms across her chest. "I've never heard Buddy bark so much."

"It's Sweetie," Charles told her. "Buddy's jealous. He doesn't understand that we will always love him best."

"Hmm." Mom frowned. "That's not so good. It's important for them to get along if we're going to foster Sweetie."

"But Buddy's not being mean to her," Charles said quickly. He wouldn't be able to stand it if they had to give up on fostering the tiny poodle. He loved to watch her scamper around. "I think he just needs some time to get to know Sweetie."

Mom nodded. "You're probably right. Anyway, it's time for dinner. Let's put Sweetie into the puppy crate for now and let her settle in a bit.

Maybe by tomorrow Buddy will get used to having her around."

Charles and Lizzie and the Bean tried to give Buddy lots of attention that night. They fed him special treats and patted him constantly, and Charles even read to him from Buddy's favorite book, *Three Stories You Can Read to Your Dog*. But tonight Buddy did not seem to be paying attention. Instead, he kept one eye on Sweetie as she wandered around the living room. And he barked every time she went near one of the Petersons. Finally, Sweetie curled up on a pillow near the fireplace and fell asleep, and only then did Buddy relax on Charles's lap.

Buddy slept in Lizzie's room that night, and Dad put Sweetie's crate into Charles's room so she wouldn't be too lonely. Once they were alone in his room, Charles gave Sweetie all the kisses and hugs he could not give her in front of Buddy. "I'm sure everything will be fine in the morning," he told her.

But he was wrong.

A good night's sleep did not change anything, as far as Buddy was concerned. In the morning, he still thought it was just plain wrong for any of his people to play with Sweetie — and he let it be known.

After breakfast, Charles and Lizzie were in the living room with the puppies. Charles had Sweetie on his lap. He was teaching her to give him a kiss whenever he said, "Kisses!" She was such a quick learner.

At first Buddy whined and barked. "Poor Buddy!" Lizzie said. For a while she distracted him with a rubber tug toy, but soon he gave up on playing with that. Now he lay with his head on his paws and watched Charles and Sweetie with a sad look on his face.

"Buddy, come on." Lizzie dangled Mr. Duck in front of him. Usually Buddy loved to grab the fuzzy stuffed toy and dash around the room with it, shaking it madly. But today he only glanced at

Mr. Duck, then sighed and dropped his head back to his paws.

"Poor Buddy," said Charles. "Maybe I should take Sweetie away for a while. Sammy and I were supposed to go over to David's today anyway. Maybe I can take her with me."

David sounded unsure when Charles called to ask if Sweetie could come over. "I don't know. I can't wait to meet your new foster puppy. But what about Slinky? I'll call you back," he said.

Slinky was David's cat. She was so shy that, so far, Charles and Sammy had never even seen her. David said Slinky mostly hid under the couch when company was around. Sammy thought Slinky might be David's imaginary pet. But Charles believed in her. He had seen a picture of Slinky on David's bulletin board. She was really pretty, with brown and black coloring. Tortoiseshell, David called it.

A few minutes later, David phoned back to say it was okay to bring Sweetie over. "But Mom says we have to kind of smuggle her into the basement, so Slinky doesn't know there's a puppy in the house."

"That'll be easy," said Charles. "Sweetie is so small I could practically put her in my pocket."

Charles's dad drove the boys over to David's. Sweetie rode in her crate in the back of the van, but when they arrived, Charles tucked her into his backpack. At first she wriggled and whined, but when Charles petted her, she settled down. She looked so cute with her curly head poking out and her bright eyes shining.

David met them at the front door with his finger over his lips. "Shh," he said. "Slinky's in the living room." The boys tiptoed to the basement door and slipped downstairs. Only then did Charles let Sweetie out of his backpack. She leapt out, light as a feather, and shook herself just like Buddy always did after a bath. She blinked at the boys.

Well, hello. A new audience for my tricks!

"She's tiny!" said David.

"Tiny? She's minuscule." Sammy bent down to pet her. "Hi there, Sweetie."

"Wait'll you see this." Charles sat on the bottom step and patted his knee. "Up, Sweetie!" She bounded over and leapt onto his knee. "Kisses!" he said. He lowered his head so she could lick his cheek.

"Wow!" David sat down on the weight bench. "Will she jump onto my lap?"

"Try it," Charles said.

"Up, Sweetie!" David patted his lap. In a flash, Sweetie was sitting there, her ears perked up and her tail wagging. "Man!" said David. "If I could jump like that, I would be in the Olympics!"

Then Sammy had to try. Sweetie jumped into his lap, too.

"This dog should be in the circus," said Sammy.

David came over to pet Sweetie. "This dog *could* be in the circus," he said. "If my cousin adopted her!"

CHAPTER FIVE

"What are you talking about?" Sammy asked.

"My cousin Ducky. He's in the circus, and he'll be here in two weeks!" David's eyes sparkled. "His circus is doing a show in the city, and he's staying with us for three whole days."

Sammy looked over at Charles, eyebrows raised. Charles knew what that meant. Sammy thought this was another of David's wild stories. "The circus, huh?" Sammy asked. "What, is he an acrobat or something? A lion tamer?"

David shook his head. "Ducky's a juggler."

"Really?" asked Charles. He had always wanted to learn to juggle. His dad could juggle three oranges. He made it look easy, but when Charles tried, he always dropped the oranges so that they rolled all over the kitchen floor and got mushy, which didn't make Mom too happy. Dad had tried to teach Charles, but so far Charles just didn't get it. "That's cool."

"I know," said David. "Ducky *is* cool. You should see what he can do. Once I saw him juggle seven golf balls. Or sometimes he juggles whatever is near him, like a hammer, a coffee mug, and a pillow. And he can palm a basketball in each hand, and do magic tricks, and eat fire!"

Charles noticed that Sammy's eyebrows shot up a little higher each time David said something about Ducky. So what if Sammy didn't believe David? Charles couldn't wait to hear more.

"He's amazing," David finished. "And he's really nice, too. He loves animals, and they love him. Even Slinky will sit in his lap to get petted."

"Do you really think he would adopt Sweetie? A circus would be the perfect place for her." Charles could just picture Sweetie in the spotlight, in the middle of a three-ring circus under a colorful tent. She would wear a shiny crown and maybe a sparkly costume, and she would jump through hoops, do tricks, maybe even ride bareback on a horse. Smart little Sweetie could probably learn to do anything. And the audience would clap and cheer and throw flowers to the newest star. Charles patted his knee. "Up, Sweetie!" The tiny dog ran over and jumped onto his lap. "What do you think?" he asked her. "Want to join the circus?"

Sweetie looked up at him with bright, shiny eyes.

Whatever you're asking, the answer is yes, yes, yes!

She wriggled and squirmed and nibbled on Charles's chin.

Charles giggled. "I think that's a yes," he said.

36

Sammy rolled his eyes. "Whatever." He grabbed the boodja and the blat. "How about some base-boodja?"

Charles could tell that Sammy wanted to change the subject. He obviously did not believe that David had a cousin who was in the circus. And he did not like it when David got all the attention with one of his wild stories.

"I have an even better idea." David jumped up onto the weight bench and began to inch along it like a tightrope walker, holding his arms out for balance. "Let's play circus!"

Charles glanced at Sammy. Sammy was frowning, and Charles knew why. Sammy liked to be the one who had great ideas. But circus sounded like a blast. "Okay!" said Charles. "I get to be the animal trainer. Come on, Salami. It'll be fun."

"I'm a juggler and an acrobat." David jumped down off the weight bench.

"And I'm the ringmaster!" Sammy finally gave

in. "That means I do all the announcing, plus I'll be in all the acts." He held up a pretend microphone to his mouth. "Ladeeez and gentleworms," he shouted. "Preeesenting, for the first time anywhere, Sweetie! The world's most talented puppy!" He turned to Sweetie. "Give her a big hand, folks."

David and Charles clapped and whooped. Then Charles grabbed a hula hoop that was leaning against the treadmill. He held it up in front of Sweetie. "And now, for her first trick, Sweetie will jump through this hoop —"

Almost before he had finished his sentence, Sweetie leapt right through the hoop.

For a second, all three boys were speechless.

"Whoa," Sammy said finally. "That was awesome."

"Let's do it again." Charles held up the hoop. Sweetie jumped through it as if she'd been doing it every day of her life. He couldn't believe it.

"Now let's have her land on my back." David dropped to his hands and knees in front of the hula hoop. "Up, Sweetie!" he said.

"Wait —" said Charles. He wasn't sure that was such a good idea. But before he could stop her, Sweetie sailed from her spot on the floor right through the hoop, landing perfectly on David's back.

Charles and Sammy burst into cheers and applause.

Sweetie stood there with her head cocked.

Thank you, thank you!

Then she jumped off David's back and ran back to Charles. He scooped her up in his arms. "You're amazing, Sweetie." He gave her a big kiss.

"That was so cool." David jumped to his feet.

"I can't believe she did that." Sammy shook his head.

David and Sammy clustered around Charles, reaching out to pat Sweetie.

"Think she can do it again?" Sammy stepped back and pretended to speak into the microphone. "Once more, watch the Stupendous Sweetie jump through the hoop of flames!"

David ran back to his position and kneeled on the floor. Charles put Sweetie down and held up the hoop. "Up, Sweetie!" called David, and she did it again.

Maybe Sweetie really *was* the most talented puppy in the world.

For the rest of the afternoon, the boys tried every trick they could think of. They did somersaults while Sweetie jumped over them. They stood in a line, front to back with their legs apart, and Sweetie ran through the tunnel they made. They taught her to sit up pretty on her hind legs, and Charles was sure that with a little more work she would be able to take a few steps on her hind feet.

Charles had a feeling that if David really did have a cousin in the circus, he would adopt Sweetie in a minute. And if David's cousin didn't exist, even Sammy still had to agree: Circus with Sweetie was the best game ever — maybe even better than base-boodja.

CHAPTER SIX

Every day after school that week, Mom drove Sammy and Charles and Sweetie over to David's.

Every day she said the same thing to David's mother — "Are you *sure* it's okay?" — and explained again about how poor Buddy was having a hard time adjusting to life with Sweetie.

Every day David's mother said that it was fine, and that the boys were welcome as long as they didn't bother the cat. She promised to check in often to make sure the boys weren't "roughhousing too much down there."

And every day Charles and Sammy and David and Sweetie played circus.

They were getting really good. Sweetie was practically ready to join a real circus. Charles had not told anyone in his family yet, but he was pretty sure that David's cousin would end up adopting Sweetie. When they found out, everybody would be so happy. Especially Buddy. He was getting a little better about having Sweetie around, but he still barked if he saw her perched on Charles's lap, and sulked if he saw Lizzie pet her.

The circus game started the same way every day. "Ladeeez and gentlepups," Sammy announced. He had made a ringmaster's tall top hat out of black construction paper and a megaphone out of red. "Welcome to the Sam-Char-Da Circus!" (He had made that name up by combining their three names. Charles did not think it was the best circus name ever, but he kept that to himself.) "For your entertainment, we present this evening our star performer,

43

that delightful dog, that perfect puppy, that completely clever canine: Sweetie the poodle!"

Charles walked out into the middle of the mat-covered floor with Sweetie trotting next to him on a red leash. "Take a bow, Sweetie," he said as he bowed down himself, and Sweetie copied him. She stuck her two tiny front paws out and stretched in a doggy play pose.

Charles had recently seen Lizzie teach Buddy to "take a bow" just by saying those words whenever he stretched that way, and then giving him a treat for a reward. Soon Buddy learned to bow whenever he heard the command. So Charles had taught Sweetie, too. It was the perfect trick for a circus dog. Every time she did it, the crowd (Charles, David, and Sammy) went wild.

Then the tricks began. Sweetie could already shake hands, bark on command, sit up pretty, and even take three or four steps on her hind feet. Charles ran through all her tricks with her and then moved on to the really flashy stuff. Sweetie was getting better and better at jumping through the hoop, even if he held it up really high.

Charles could tell that Sweetie loved every minute of it. She loved doing the tricks, she loved the attention and the applause, and she loved the treats and the kisses and hugs she got every time she did something special. She was so happy that sometimes she just dashed around in wild circles with her eyes shining and her fluffy ears flapping wildly. She barked and barked and wagged her tail and barked some more.

This is the most fun I've ever had. I was born to be a performer!

"Boys!" David's mom came down the stairs to check up on them. "Try not to get Sweetie overexcited. Slinky can hear the barking and it makes her nervous." She gave David a look. "I hope you boys aren't up to anything dangerous," she said.

All three boys shook their heads. What could be dangerous about playing circus?

On Thursday afternoon, David mentioned that his cousin would be arriving in a few days.

"We need a really special trick, to knock his socks off," said Sammy.

They all thought for a few minutes. "Got it." David snapped his fingers. "Let's make a human pyramid."

Charles didn't know what that meant until David explained. "We used to do it at my camp last summer. You guys get on your hands and knees, next to each other. Then I'll climb up so that one of my hands and one of my knees is on each of your backs."

"Why do you get to be on top?" Sammy asked.

"I'm the littlest," David said.

Sammy and Charles looked at each other and shrugged. "Okay," said Charles, even though

46

he wondered if this might be what David's mother called roughhousing. "C'mon, Salami." He dropped to his hands and knees. Sammy did the same, right next to Charles. Then David climbed on top. David's bony knee dug into Charles's back. But when Charles raised his head to glance in the mirror, he could not believe how totally cool they looked.

"Now let's see if Sweetie will climb up on top of me," David said.

"I don't know —" Charles began, but David was already calling the puppy.

"Sweetie, up!" he said.

Sweetie ran over and jumped, and Charles felt her step lightly on his back for just a moment before she scrambled up onto David's.

"Whoa!" Sammy checked the mirror. "This is the best trick yet."

"This rocks!" David agreed.

"Except that my back is killing me. I can't hold you up anymore." Charles groaned and sank onto his belly. His face was squashed into the plastic-smelling mat. David tumbled onto the mat, laughing, and Sweetie sprang off and landed as lightly as a leaf. A second later, she licked Charles's face.

Wake up, sleepyhead!

The pyramid was the coolest circus trick yet. They practiced it over and over. Charles put on a thick sweatshirt so that David's knees wouldn't stick into him so badly. Sammy made up a whole speech about the Amaaaazing, One-of-a-Kind, Never-Before-Seen Human Pyramid Topped by a Poodle! And David kept coming up with ideas to make the pyramid better and better.

They were trying one out, with David *standing* on their backs, one foot on Charles and one foot on Sammy. He had just called Sweetie to see if she would jump into his arms, when the door at the top of the stairs popped open.

"It's a little *too* quiet down there." David's mother started down the stairs, a dish towel in her hand. "What are you boys up to?"

But before she made it down far enough to see them, something else happened. Charles saw a flash of brown on the stairs near her feet. He heard a startled yowl. Slinky! The cat's curiosity must have gotten the better of her. Sweetie took off toward the stairs, chasing madly after the terrified cat.

"Whoaaa," David cried as he lost his balance. He fell backward, and Charles heard a dull clunk.

When Charles jumped up and turned around, he saw David lying on the floor near the treadmill, holding his head in his hands. "Oww!" wailed David as his mother rushed down the last few steps.

"Are you okay, honey?" she cried.

David reached out for her. "Mom!"

Then Charles saw the blood.

CHAPTER SEVEN

David's mom knelt at his side and held the dish towel to his bleeding head. Sammy knelt, too, and patted David's shoulder. Charles stared at them. He felt as if he'd been frozen in a block of ice, like he couldn't move his hands or feet. Wasn't there something he could do?

David moaned.

"Charles! Go upstairs and call nine-one-one," said David's mother.

Of course. He should have thought of that before. He forgot about being frozen and dashed to the stairs. He started up, taking them two at a time.

"Take it slow, Charles!" called David's mother. "We don't need another accident."

Charles slowed down a teensy bit. Upstairs, he ran to the kitchen phone. Way back when he was the Bean's age, his dad had taught Charles about calling 911. Dad had always told him that for real, true emergencies when you needed help fast, dialing 911 was the best way to call the police, or firefighters, or an ambulance. He knew that you should never call 911 just for fun or as an experiment to see what would happen. But this was definitely an emergency. So for the very first time, Charles was about to punch those numbers into a telephone.

He took a deep breath to calm himself down, the way Dad had taught him. He got ready to listen, because he knew that the dispatcher, the person who answered the phone, would have some questions for him. Then he punched in the three numbers: 9-1-1.

Later it was hard to remember everything he had said. He knew he had told the dispatcher that there had been an accident, that his friend had hit his head on something. He knew he had told her David's address (that was easy to remember, because it rhymed: 42 Meadow View) and phone number. By the time he'd answered her questions, she'd told him that help was already on its way.

Sure enough, only a few moments after he hung up, he heard a siren coming closer. Charles ran to the front door so he could wave to the ambulance and let them know they were at the right house. His heart pounded.

The ambulance pulled up in front of the house, and three people in blue jumpsuits piled out. Charles knew all of them. They were firefighters from his dad's station. Like his dad, they didn't just fight fires. They were also EMTs, emergency medical technicians, who were trained to take care of medical emergencies. If Dad had been on duty that afternoon, he might have been there, too.

"Charles!" Meg Parker was the first one up the porch steps. "Are you okay?"

Charles nodded. "I'm fine. But my friend David fell and hit his head."

"Show me where he is." Meg was all business.

The two other EMTs, Andy and Scott, ran up. Andy had a big orange duffel bag slung over one shoulder, and Scott carried what looked like a long blue surfboard. Charles led them all down to the basement, and without any extra talking they knelt around David and began to check him out.

"That was fast," Sammy whispered to Charles. He cradled Sweetie in his arms, and his face was pale. Even Sweetie seemed to know that something serious was going on. She didn't wriggle or struggle, and when Sammy handed her to Charles, she just quietly licked his face and then settled down in his arms. Charles took her leash out of his pocket and clipped it onto her collar, just in case. They did not need a poodle puppy running around.

David's mom stood and watched the EMTs. Her face was even whiter than Sammy's.

Finally, Meg rose to her feet. "David is going to be just fine," she said. "He's got a nasty cut that may need some stitches, and since he did hit his head, we'll move him very carefully. We'll use the backboard to carry him up the stairs." She gestured to Scott, who laid the surfboard thing down next to David.

Charles inched a little closer so he could watch. The EMTs worked fast. They bandaged the top of David's head in white gauze and strapped him to the board. At one point, he opened his eyes and looked straight at Charles. David did not look scared. In fact, he even gave Charles a little smile. "Take care of Sweetie," he said.

"I will." Charles gave Sweetie a kiss on the head as he and Sammy watched the EMTs carry David up the stairs. David's mother followed close behind. Suddenly, Charles thought of something. David was on his way to the hospital — and his mom would go, too, which would leave Sammy and Charles alone at the house. "Maybe I should call my mom to come get us," he said to Sammy.

But when they got upstairs, there was Charles's dad, already talking to Meg. He ran over to Charles, knelt down, and gave him a big strong bear hug. "David's going to be fine," he whispered into Charles's ear. "I'm so glad you're safe. When my beeper went off and I heard there was an ambulance on its way to this address —" He stopped and shook his head. "I'm just glad everyone's okay."

The EMTs put David into the back of the ambulance and drove off with their lights flashing. David's mother followed in her car.

Charles and his dad and Sammy just stood there for a moment, without talking. Charles realized that his legs felt shaky. Then he realized something else: Sweetie wanted to get down and run around.

She gave a little bark and began to wriggle in Charles's arms. He put her down on the ground. "You were a very, very good girl," he said.

"You did pretty well yourself." Dad ruffled Charles's hair. "I'm proud of you."

Later, when Mom heard the whole story, she was proud, too. But at dinner that night, she also gave Charles quite a lecture about being more careful. "This is exactly why I worry about you boys getting too wild," she said. "You can be having fun one minute, and the next minute somebody can wind up —"

Luckily, just then the phone rang. It was David's mother. "Everything is okay," she told Charles. "David had some stitches in his head, so he looks like Frankenstein's monster, and they want to keep him at the hospital overnight just to keep an eye on him — but he feels fine. I'm going to pick him up in the morning, and I thought you and Sammy might like to come along."

"Definitely," said Charles. "That would be great."

"And, Charles" — David's mother's voice grew softer — "thanks. You really helped out."

CHAPTER EIGHT

"Maybe we should forget about the circus game and go back to boodja-ball." David smiled weakly. "It's safer."

It was the next morning, and Sammy and Charles stood near the bed in David's hospital room while his mom talked to a nurse just outside the door. Charles shifted from foot to foot, feeling uncomfortable. It was weird to see David lying there with a big white bandage on his head. Charles was half disappointed and half relieved that he could not see David's stitches. He wasn't sure what to say or how to act. He had not spent a lot of time in hospitals before. He looked at Sammy. Maybe Sammy would think of something to say.

Sammy stared down at the floor.

"Boodja-ball sounds good," said Charles. "Um, I'm sorry you got hurt."

"It's not your fault," David said. "I'm the one who came up with the whole crazy idea to stand on your backs." He grinned. "Anyway, I'm fine. I'm just happy I get to go home. The food here is terrible." He pointed at a tray on a table next to his bed. "They call that French toast?"

Sammy perked up. "French toast?"

"You can have it if you want it," said David. "I couldn't eat it."

Sammy went over and started to poke at the leftover breakfast.

Charles shook his head. Sammy would eat anything.

David's mom came into the room. "Ready to go home?" She ruffled David's hair. "As soon as the nurse says you're free to leave, we'll get you out of here."

"All right!" said David.

There was a knock at the door. "Hello?" A smiling redheaded woman with a freckled nose leaned into the room. She gave a little wave. "It looks as if you already have visitors — want another?" She gestured to a big curly-haired brown dog who stood next to her. "I'm Jamie, and this is Tate. He's a therapy dog and he loves to visit people in the hospital."

Charles recognized Jamie right away. She was the puppy kindergarten teacher! He had met her when he and Lizzie had taken Rascal, a wild little puppy they had fostered, to her class. Jamie was a great dog trainer: patient and caring and always ready to crack a joke.

"Cool!" said David. "Come on in, Tate."

Tate trotted right into the room and headed straight for David's bed. He put his front paws up on the bed, very gently, and let David pat him.

"He'll give you a kiss if you ask for one," Jamie said. She smiled encouragingly at David.

"How about a kiss, Tate?" asked David. Tate

leaned forward and nuzzled David's cheek. He looked huge compared to Sweetie.

Charles couldn't believe there was a dog in the hospital. Lizzie had told him about therapy dogs who were trained to visit people in hospitals and nursing homes, but he had never met one before. "Can we pet Tate?" he asked Jamie.

Jamie turned to look at him. "Hey, I know you. Charles, right? Your family fosters puppies. You brought one to my puppy kindergarten class." She grinned and shook her head. "Rascal. That Jack Russell terrier was one of the few dogs I have ever had to kick out of class. But I know you found him a great home anyway." She gestured to Tate. "Of course you can pet him. Tate loves attention."

Charles and Sammy went over and knelt down by Tate. His fur was curly and soft, and he held perfectly still while they petted him. Then he put out his big paw for a shake. "He's so good," Charles said.

"Tate is the best," Jamie said proudly. Charles could tell how much she loved her dog. "That's partly his personality and partly his training. Therapy dogs have to be friendly, but not *too* friendly — we don't want them to jump on sick people, or kiss people who don't like dogs. They have to have good manners, too. Tate is perfect for the job."

"What's the idea behind therapy dogs?" asked David's mother. She came over to pet Tate.

"Having a dog come to visit can really lift some people's spirits, if they are lonely or sad in the hospital," Jamie said. "Dogs love everyone, whether they are sick or well, old or young. And most people are happy to be around a dog. A visit gives people something to look forward to. You should see the smiles when Tate and I go to the nursing home. He reminds a lot of older people of the dogs they used to have. Plus, he gives people something to think about besides being sick or lonely or hurting."

"Does Tate have special training?" David's mom asked.

"Oh, yes," said Jamie. "Besides all the manners I've taught him, and the tricks he knows, he also had to learn how to behave on visits and pass a special test before he became a certified therapy dog. Training Tate to be a therapy dog was one of the most challenging and enjoyable things I've ever done."

Charles fingered the tag on Tate's collar that said THERAPY DOG.

"What kind of dog is Tate?" asked Sammy.

"He's a mutt, a mixed-breed. I think he has some poodle in him. That would explain the curly hair, and why he's so smart."

"We know a miniature poodle puppy who is *really* smart," said David. "She can do a ton of tricks. And she makes everybody smile."

"She could probably become a good therapy dog, when she grows up." Jamie clucked her tongue. "Tate, can you show us some tricks?"

Tate could sit, shake hands, roll over, and sit up pretty. But his best trick was when Jamie pretended to sneeze with a big "Ah-choo!" Tate trotted over to a tissue box, pulled out a tissue with his teeth, and brought it to her. David and Sammy and Charles liked that trick so much that they all had to have a turn pretending to sneeze so that Tate could bring them a tissue.

Then, just as Jamie was showing them how Tate could play dead, a nurse came in. "You're all set, David. You can head home anytime."

Charles was surprised. He'd had so much fun watching Tate that he'd almost forgotten he was in the hospital. Maybe that was what therapy dogs were all about.

They each gave Tate a hug and said good-bye to him and Jamie. Then Charles and Sammy waited out in the hall while David got dressed and ready to go.

"I've got a big surprise for you," David's mom

told him on the way home. "Ducky's coming tomorrow."

"Tomorrow? I thought he wasn't coming until next week," David said.

"He wasn't — until he heard about your accident. He said he figured you could use some cheering up."

"Cool." David grinned. "I hope he remembers not to wear his costume."

His mom laughed.

"What costume?" Charles asked.

"His clown outfit," said David. "Didn't I tell you? Ducky is a clown. But he never wears his costume when he visits, because my dad —" He laughed. "Well, believe it or not, my dad thinks clowns are scary."

Charles looked at Sammy.

Sammy looked back at Charles.

Sammy was the only person in the whole world who knew Charles's secret: He, too, was afraid of clowns.

65

CHAPTER NINE

"It'll be okay, Cheese," Sammy said as he and Charles stood outside David's front door the next day, waiting for someone to answer the doorbell. Charles glanced down at the puppy in his arms. He hoped more than anything that David's cousin Ducky would want to adopt Sweetie. That was the plan, wasn't it? The whole reason they had practiced all those circus routines?

But now that he knew Ducky was a clown, Charles was nervous about meeting him. In fact, he was so worried about it that he had barely slept a wink the night before. What was it about clowns? Charles had never liked them. Their scary white faces and big red mouths . . . their alarmingly bright, baggy costumes . . . their terrifying giant shoes . . . And the hair! That bright yellow or orange hair that stuck out in crazy directions! It could give you nightmares.

"He won't be dressed in his costume," Sammy reminded Charles. "No makeup either, I'm sure."

"I know." Charles looked down at his hands. He should probably be embarrassed that Sammy knew his secret, but really it just felt good to know that his best friend would be there when he met his first real, live clown in person. "Thanks, Salami," he added. There was nothing like an old friend you could trust with your secrets.

The door flew open. "Hey there. You must be Sammy and Charles. And that's Sweetie! She's even cuter than David's description."

Charles stared at the person who had opened the door. He had the hugest hands and feet Charles had ever seen and a smile so wide you could practically see his back teeth. His ears stuck straight out from his head, and his curly red hair was wild and unruly. He wore sneakers, jeans, and a black T-shirt that said CLANCY'S CIRCUS in red block letters.

"I'm Ducky." He stuck out a gigantic hand for a shake.

Charles took it. Ducky's hand swallowed up his hand whole. Charles knew he should say, "I'm Charles," but he couldn't seem to get the words out.

"I know, I know, I look like a clown even *without* my costume." Ducky grinned a wide grin as he shook Sammy's hand. "Guess I'm a natural for the job." He let out a big belly laugh.

And then, just like that, Charles couldn't help laughing, too. There was something about Ducky that just made you want to smile and laugh. Maybe he *was* a natural for the job. And maybe — just maybe! — all clowns weren't so scary once you knew them.

David appeared behind Ducky. "Hi," he said. He looked almost back to normal, except for the bandage on his head. "Let's go downstairs and show Ducky our big surprise."

The boys had agreed that David would not tell Ducky that Sweetie needed a forever home. They wanted him to see her in action. Then he would know that she was perfect for the circus.

Down in the basement, Charles put Sweetie on the floor so she could run around for a while. Ducky spotted the Nerf ball and the Wiffle bat. He picked them up, looked around the room, grabbed the hula hoop, and started to juggle the three completely different items. "Yee-haw!" he yelled. "Oops! Duck!" The Wiffle bat flew straight at Charles.

Charles ducked as the bat flew over his head.

Ducky laughed. "That's how I got my nickname," he said. "In clown school, I was always losing track of something I was juggling. They started calling me Ducky after I yelled, 'Duck!' one too many times."

"Clown school?" Charles had never heard of that. An hour ago he would have thought clown school sounded like the scariest place in the world, but now he wasn't so sure. In fact, as Ducky started to tell the boys more about it, clown school sounded like a pretty cool place.

At clown school Ducky had learned more than how to juggle. He'd learned how to walk on a tightrope, and how to drive a funny little car, and how to do twenty somersaults in a row without getting dizzy. "Oh, and I learned some magic, too." He reached down to ruffle Sweetie's ears and pulled a nickel out of one of them. Then he flipped the nickel into the air, and it turned into a dime. Then he closed his hand over the dime, and when he opened it back up again, there were three dimes! He gave one to each of the boys.

"Wow," said Sammy.

David beamed. "And you didn't even believe that my cousin was in the circus," he said.

"I — I —" Sammy blushed. "Well, I do now."

Ducky picked up the Wiffle bat again and pointed it at the white wipe-off board. "What's a Grand Boodjerino?" he asked.

The boys explained about base-boodja.

"Pitch to me," Ducky said. "Let me try."

Sweetie perched on the weight bench to watch as the boys took up their positions and David pitched to his cousin. *Bam!* On the very first swing, Ducky connected and the boodja screamed past the rowing machine. "I did it! I did it!" Ducky picked Sweetie up and danced her around happily as the boys cheered his Grand Boodjerino.

Then Ducky put his hand over his mouth. "Oops. Your mom said we were supposed to take it easy down here. We promised her that David would sit down and stay quiet after his night in the hospital."

"Let's do our show," said Charles. He and Sammy would have to do it all, but that was okay.

Sammy ran for his ringmaster's hat and megaphone while Charles grabbed the hula hoop and got Sweetie ready to do her tricks.

"Ladeeez and gentleclowns!" Sammy announced. "Welcome to the greatest show on earth! Meet Sweetie, the amazingly acrobatic wonder dog!"

Charles held up the hoop. "Up, Sweetie!" he said, and Sweetie sailed through the hoop. Then Sammy got on his hands and knees and Sweetie jumped through again, right up onto Sammy's back.

"Woo-hoo!" Ducky yelled and clapped.

They ran through all Sweetie's tricks, or at least the ones they could do without David. They explained about the human pyramid, and how Sweetie could climb all the way to the top.

"She really is a wonder dog," said Ducky. He scooped up Sweetie and gave her a big hug and kiss. She licked his chin.

I'm glad you liked the show!

It was now or never. "She needs a home. Would you like to adopt her?" asked Charles. "She could be the star of your circus."

"Great idea," said Ducky, "except for one thing. My circus doesn't have any animals in it."

Charles stared at him. "What do you mean?" he asked. "Circuses always have animals. Horses, lions, elephants . . . isn't that part of what a circus is?"

"Not necessarily," said Ducky. He was still petting Sweetie. "A lot of people believe now that circuses are not the best places for wild animals, or tame ones, either. Milton Clancy, who runs my circus, feels that way. Our circus is all people: jugglers, acrobats, tightrope walkers, and clowns."

"Maybe you could adopt Sweetie anyway, just as a pet," said Charles. He still thought Ducky would be the perfect owner for Sweetie.

Ducky shook his head. "I don't think she'd be very happy living in my one-room trailer and traveling every other day to a new town." He gave Sweetie one more kiss. Then he flashed that huge grin at Charles. "Don't look so disappointed," he said. "There must be somebody around who would want to adopt such a smart, funny dog."

CHAPTER TEN

Dad cooked up a big pot of firehouse-style chili and Mom made a salad. Charles set the table. Lizzie vacuumed the living room while Buddy and Sweetie chased the vacuum everywhere it went. They played together all the time now, and Buddy didn't even seem to notice anymore when Sweetie was close to one of his people. Even the Bean had a job: He went around and collected all of Buddy's dog toys, then put them into the big basket where they belonged.

The Petersons were having a Valentine's Day party, in honor of Sweetie.

On the guest list were:

•David and Sammy
•Ducky

- Rick the rookie
- and last, but not least, Jamie, the therapy-dog lady.

After Ducky had explained why he couldn't adopt Sweetie, Charles had come up with another idea. He remembered Jamie and her excellent dog, Tate. Jamie was a dog trainer. Maybe she would know somebody who was looking for a puppy.

With Mom's help, Charles found Jamie's phone number and called her up. After he said hello and reminded her who he was, he said, "Remember that miniature poodle puppy we told you about? You said she might be a good therapy dog when she's older?"

Jamie remembered.

"Well," said Charles, "my family is fostering that puppy. Her name is Sweetie, and as a matter of fact, she needs a home."

"Well," said Jamie, "as a matter of fact, I might know someone who's looking for a puppy."

With his mom's permission, Charles invited Jamie over for dinner the next night so she could meet Sweetie. Then he thought it might be good to have Sammy and David come, too, so they could show off Sweetie's tricks. And of course Ducky had to be invited, too, since Charles had told his family all about him and they wanted to meet the famous juggler. Then Dad asked if Rick could come, because Rick was still kind of sad about breaking up with his girlfriend, plus he missed Sweetie and would love to see her.

Now the house was clean, the chili simmered on the stove, and the table was set. Party time!

Rick was the first to arrive. He trudged in gloomily, but he beamed when Sweetie scampered over to greet him. "Hey there, little girl." He scooped her up into his big arms.

Sweetie wriggled happily and shook her fluffy ears.

I remember you!

"Wait till you see all the tricks she's learned," Charles told him.

"I always knew she was a smart one," said Rick. He petted the top of Sweetie's head.

Next came David and Ducky.

"Can you really find nickels in people's ears?" Lizzie asked Ducky.

As an answer, Ducky peered into Lizzie's ear. "No nickels today." But he pulled something out. "Will a quarter do?" He held up a quarter.

The Bean stared. "Look in my ear!" he demanded.

Ducky knelt down and checked the Bean's ear. "Nothing in this one," he said. He checked the other one. "Well, look at that." He pulled out another quarter, flipped it high into the air, caught it, and handed it to the Bean. Mom took it from him before he could put it into his mouth.

Everybody was clapping when the doorbell rang again. This time it was Jamie. "Wow, it's a party," she said. "I brought Tate with me, but maybe I should leave him in the car."

"The more, the merrier, as long as he gets along with Buddy and Sweetie," said Dad. "Bring him in and we'll see how it goes."

Sammy showed up just as Buddy, Sweetie, and Tate were romping around the living room, getting to know each other. The two bigger dogs looked like giants next to Sweetie, but they were gentle with her. "Maybe I should go get Rufus and Goldie, too," Sammy suggested.

"Um, I don't think so," Mom said quickly. "We're just about to have dinner."

They sat down and ate until everybody was full, and then, because everything was so delicious, they ate some more. Then Mom brought out a special surprise: brownies and ice cream. Charles noticed that Rick scooped Jamie's ice cream for her, and that Jamie saved Rick a seat when they moved into the living room after dessert. Rick looked happier than he had for a while.

Afterward, Charles asked everyone to get ready for a show. Out in the hallway, Sammy put on his top hat and grabbed his megaphone. Charles tied a sparkly pink ribbon around Sweetie's neck. But David didn't move. He looked terrified, and Charles remembered how shy he could be in groups.

Sammy must have remembered, too. "C'mon, Donut," he said. "This is what we practiced for."

Charles could tell by David's smile that he liked his new nickname. He picked up the hula hoop he'd brought. "Ready, Salami," he said. The boys trooped into the living room.

"Ladeeeeez and chilibeans!" cried Sammy. "Welcome to the Sam-Char-Da Circus! Presenting, for your entertainment, tonight's special star, Sweetie, the amazing and adorable wonder dog!" And the show began.

Sweetie did all her tricks perfectly. She jumped through the hoop. She sat up pretty. She even walked for ten whole steps on her hind legs. The crowd went wild. Everybody clapped and clapped, except for Lizzie, who held Buddy on her lap the whole time. She petted him and talked to him in case he got jealous again when Sweetie got all the attention.

Jamie clapped hardest of all. "She's wonderful," she said when the show was over. "So cute, so smart. Sweetie is exactly the kind of dog I have been looking for."

"You?" Charles asked. "You mean *you're* the person who was looking for a dog?"

"That's right," said Jamie. "Tate and I have been wishing for another member of the family, and I think Sweetie would be the perfect addition."

"Really?" Charles felt a smile spread across his face. "You want to adopt Sweetie?"

Jamie nodded. "I'd like to train her for

therapy work, when she's old enough. Sweetie will be the star of any hospital I bring her to. And because she's a poodle, I don't have to worry as much about patients being allergic to her."

"Do you know she'll need to be groomed regularly?" Lizzie asked.

Jamie nodded. "I'm used to that. I've learned how to do it myself, because Tate needs grooming, too." Jamie reached out to pet Tate. "So, is it okay if I adopt her?"

"It's more than okay!" Charles beamed. He knew that Jamie would be a wonderful owner for Sweetie. She would train her and love her and take excellent care of her. And Sweetie would love being a therapy dog. Every day she would meet and perform for new people — people who really appreciated her. It would be even better than being a circus dog. And who knew? Judging by the way Jamie and Rick were smiling at each other, Charles thought maybe

Rick would get to be part of Sweetie's life after all.

Jamie patted her knee. "Up, Sweetie," she called. And Sweetie scampered over and leapt, as light as a feather, into her new owner's lap.

Puppy Tips

Did you know that petting a dog can make people healthier? Studies have shown that people's blood pressure goes down when they stroke a dog. That's just one of the many benefits therapy dogs bring to the people they visit.

Your dog does not have to be any special breed to be a therapy dog. Any dog over one year old can become certified to visit hospitals and nursing homes. The most important thing is for the dog to have the right personality. A good therapy dog loves to be around people. A therapy dog should be friendly, calm, confident, and gentle. Some therapy dogs do tricks or wear costumes, and others just give kisses or sit quietly with someone who needs company.

Most therapy dog organizations require a dog to pass its Canine Good Citizen test, then do some more special training and testing.

Dear Reader,

I have never had a poodle but I know that they are very special dogs. People who have poodles are crazy about them and often have more than one! My friend Annie loves her two black miniature poodles, Oggi and Pearl. They are so smart and funny and they love to curl up in your lap just like a cat would. And my friend Leda has two golden doodles, Pippa and Pogo. They love to play together. Even though they are only half poodle (the other half is golden retriever), they have to be groomed every ten weeks, just like poodles do.

Yours from the Puppy Place,
Ellen Miles

P.S. You can read more about therapy dogs, and the training they need, in *Snowball*.

THE PUPPY PLACE

DON'T MISS THE
PUPPY PLACE
SPECIAL EDITION!

Here's a peek at CHEWY AND CHICA!

What happened was this. First, there was a knock on the door. "Ms. Dobbins?" Andrew, the boy who worked at the front desk of the animal shelter, poked his head in. His cheeks were flushed pink and he stumbled over his words. "I — I think you might want to come see what just arrived."

Ms. Dobbins stood up. "Thank you, Andrew," she said.

There was something in Andrew's face that made everybody else stand up, too, and follow Ms. Dobbins out to the parking lot in front of the shelter. There Lizzie saw a big shiny black car, pulled up at an angle to the front door. The car's windows were rolled down just a bit. Lizzie couldn't believe what she was seeing, so she stepped forward to take a closer look. That car was full of puppies! Puppy noses stuck out of every window, sniffing and snuffling and snorting. Puppy paws pressed against the glass. Lizzie saw brown puppies, white puppies, and black puppies; fluffy puppies and sleek puppies; big puppies and tiny puppies. Lizzie had never seen so many puppies in one place!

The car door opened, and a tall, gangly man unfolded himself from the front seat, holding back three puppies that tried to climb out after him. He wore worn, faded overalls, with a clean white shirt underneath. He wasn't handsome — in fact, he was kind of funny-looking — but there was something about him that Lizzie liked right away. He tipped his red baseball cap and smiled at Ms. Dobbins. "Hello, ma'am," he said.

"Mr. Beauregard?" Ms. Dobbins stared at the car, and at the man, and at the puppies. "What is this?"

The man pushed back his cap, scratched his

head, and smiled shyly, and Lizzie found herself smiling back at him. "Puppies," he drawled in a southern accent. "A whole passel of puppies."

"I can see that." Ms. Dobbins turned to the others. "Mr. Beauregard is new to town but he has already become a very generous supporter of Caring Paws."

Lizzie knew what that meant. He might not look it, but this man was R-I-C-H. And he loved animals. That was good! Caring Paws always needed money for dog food and cat litter and flea shampoo and veterinarians' bills.

"These are some other friends of the shelter." Ms. Dobbins swept a hand toward the members of the Kindness Club. "And I think we *all* want to know what you're doing with a carload of puppies."

ABOUT THE AUTHOR

Ellen Miles likes to write about the different personalities of dogs. She is the author of more than 28 books, including the Puppy Place and Taylor-Made Tales series as well as *The Pied Piper* and other Scholastic Classics. Ellen loves to be outdoors every day, walking, biking, skiing, or swimming, depending on the season. She also loves to read, cook, explore her beautiful state, and hang out with friends and family. She lives in Vermont.

By the way, base-boodja is a game Ellen and her brother made up. They used to play it for hours.

If you love animals, be sure to read all the adorable stories in the Puppy Place series!

For more magical fun, be sure to
check out these tails of enchantment!